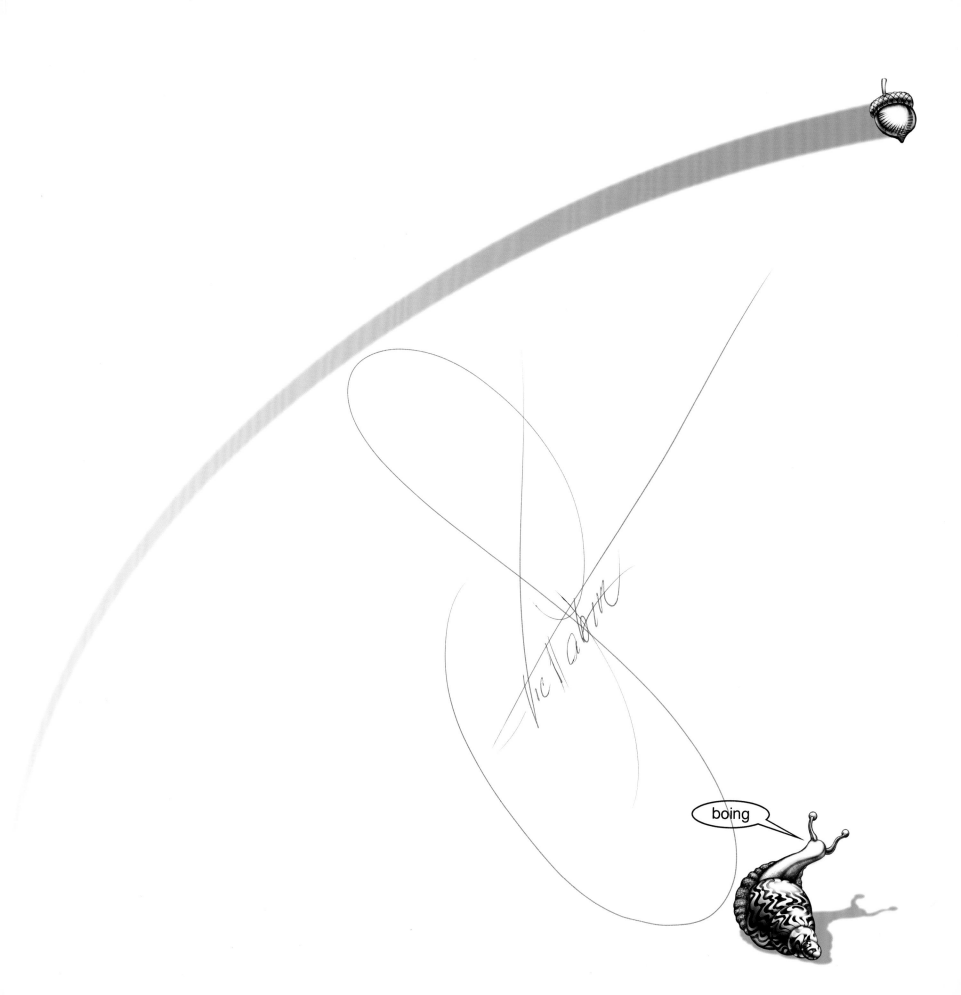

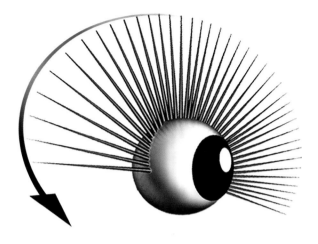

*This book is dedicated to the dictionary,*
*with special thanks for organizing*
*the universe alphabetically.*

© Victor Stabin

Published by Daedal Doodle Ink

Second Version/Edition

Printed in the United States of America

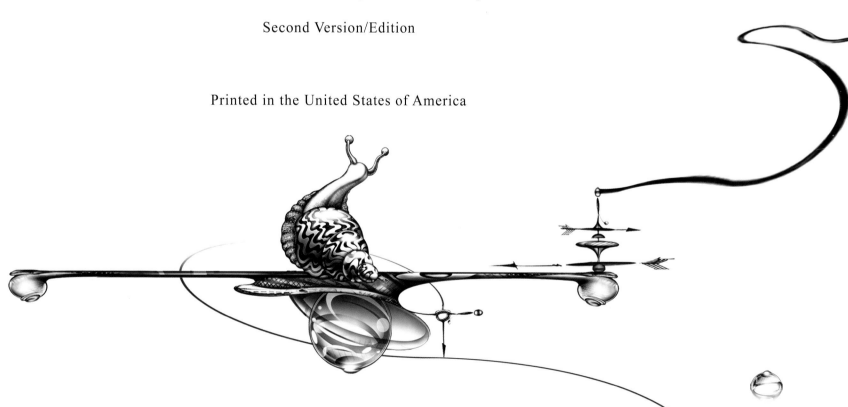

# DAEDAL DOODLE
*The ABC Book For The Ages*

# Table of Contents

# Addenda

# Dictionary as Muse

To my delight, and my wife's horror, I taught my two-year-old daughter Skyler to say "My Daddy is a megalomaniac." At the time, my wife and I were reading our children countless ABC books. At age three Skyler, went through a phase where she prefixed everything she said with "Acorn"– "Acorn Daddy," "Acorn Refrigerator," "Acorn TV," etc.

As my daughters, Arielle and Skyler, were my muses, I was inspired to create an illustration for "A is for Anti Gravity Acorn." To get to the next page (that is, "B"), I referenced the dictionary, which spawned the "Bifoliated Bonito." Initially, I thought I liked the alliteration because of the way the words bounced, but it became evident to me that the more I read the dictionary, the more I found myself discovering fascinating words that I couldn't wait to illustrate– regardless of their bounce. By the time I made it to "Eohippus's Epizoon," I understood that the dictionary had become the muse, its assignment was to find words previously unknown to me and turn them into this ABC book project. "A is for Antigravity Acorn" took it on the chin.

For three-and-a-half years, wherever I went, I brought a dictionary along. Although I didn't know who or where the audience for this effort might be, I was acutely aware of how much I loved this self-imposed task and how easy it was to stick to. My inner "Rain Man" was comforted by the lists of random words that seemed to take me across the universe alphabetically.

Having worked as an illustrator for 25 years, I always felt that part of my job was to relate to the broadest audience possible, without pandering. Though the words I found initially seemed more appropriate for adults, I knew that kids would love learning them. Not only that– parents would, too,

and they would also love hearing their children repeat them. My hero, the little acorn, might have been knocked down but not out. To keep kids wanting to turn the page, I hid acorns everywhere (except on page "F", fig fauns only like figs).

To my delight, Daedal Doodle has caught the eyes of numerous educators. Starting in the coal regions of Pennsylvania, I received grants to teach my book-making process in local high schools. I had kids create their own versions of the book, which turned their dictionaries into a curriculum for conceptual thinking and drawing. Following the PA experience, I gave a class at the Metropolitan Museum of Art. The kids were pretty much doing the same assignment, but instead of using only the dictionary, they were using the dictionary along with the museum's galleries for inspiration, (See "Afternoon at the Museum" in the addenda, pages 5-6.)

To date, I've personally sold Daedal Doodle to a pregnant woman buying the book for her unborn child, a Princeton professor who bought a dozen copies to pass around to his colleagues, a world-renowned economist who forecast its worldwide acknowledgment, to countless grandparents, and, of course, to lovers of fine books everywhere.

This 2nd version of Daedal Doodle includes addenda where I explain the book's educational component. You'll also get a glimpse of how the characters in the book are not just a bunch of pretty faces, but also have their own individual cautionary tales as media stars in the "Radio Stories." (See in the addenda pages 9-12.) The newly added sentences that accompany the alliterations were mostly* written by me with help from Skyler and Arielle. So, without further ado, ladies and germs, the sign post up ahead, submitted for your approval…

*Arielle wrote the sentence for the letter D.

*Daddy turn the page...*

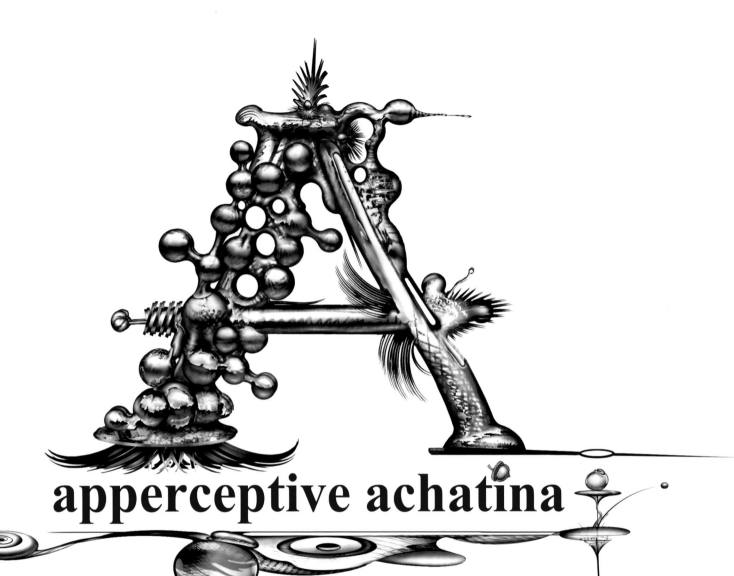

# apperceptive achatina

**Apperceptive**, /ap-er-sep-tiv/ adj. Conscious of its own consciousness; self-reflective with regard to metaphysical ends.

**Achatina**, /ak-uh-tee-nuh/ n. A giant African snail.

**Metaphysical**, /met-uh-fiz-i-kuh l/ adj. Abstract; beyond nature or the physical; supernatural.

**Shaman,** /shah-muh/ n. member of certain tribal societies who acts as a medium between the visible world and an invisible spirit world and who practices magic or sorcery for purposes of healing, divination, and control over natural events.

Slowly, the apperceptive achatina turned into a narcissistic shaman.

# bifoliate bonito

**Bifoliate**, /bahy-foh-lee-it, -eyt/ adj. Having two leaves or leaflets.

**Bonito**, /buh-nee-toh/ n. Any of several large fish of the mackerel family.

The bifoliate bonito and the oak tree were nuts about each other.

# caoutchoucoidal chelonia

**Caoutchoucoidal**, /kou-chook-oid-uh l/ adj. Made of India rubber, an elastic gum, or the dried juice of one of numerous tropical plants of the dogbane, spurge, and nettle families. Caoutchoucoidal objects are extremely elastic and impervious to water and to nearly all other fluids.
**Chelonia**, /ke-lo-ni-a/ n. Tortoises and turtles.

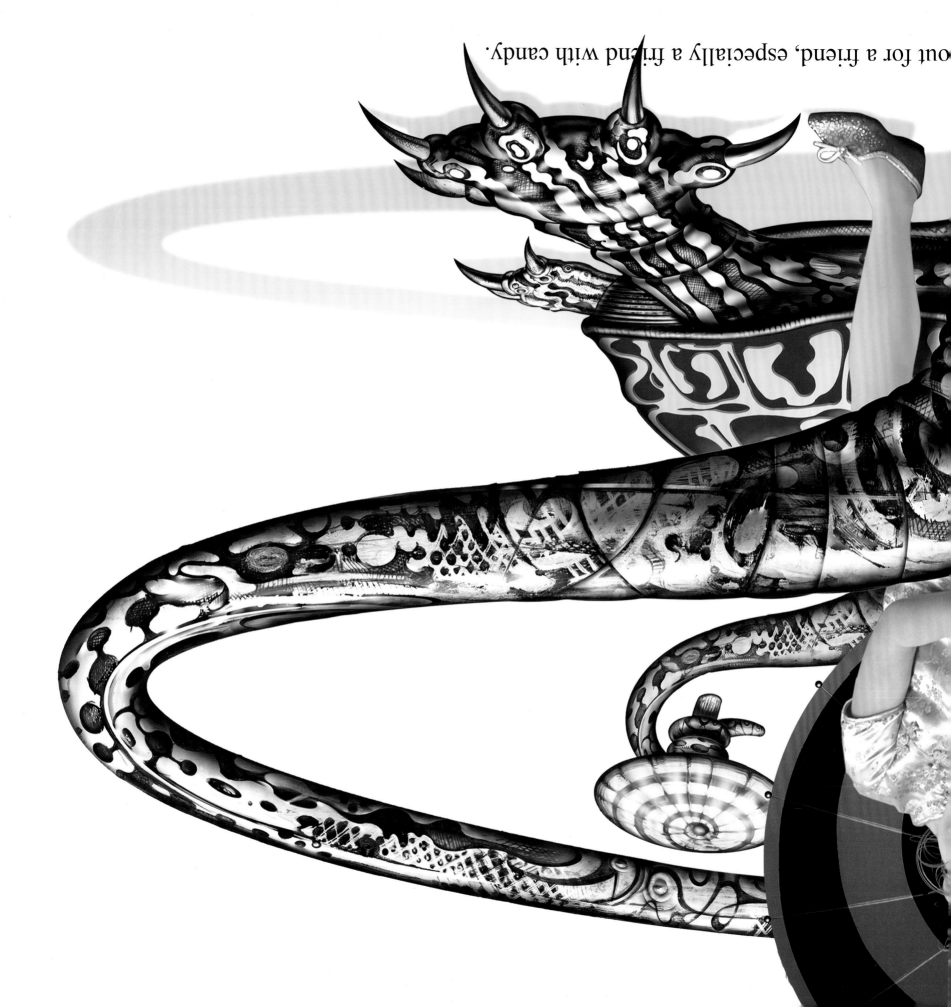

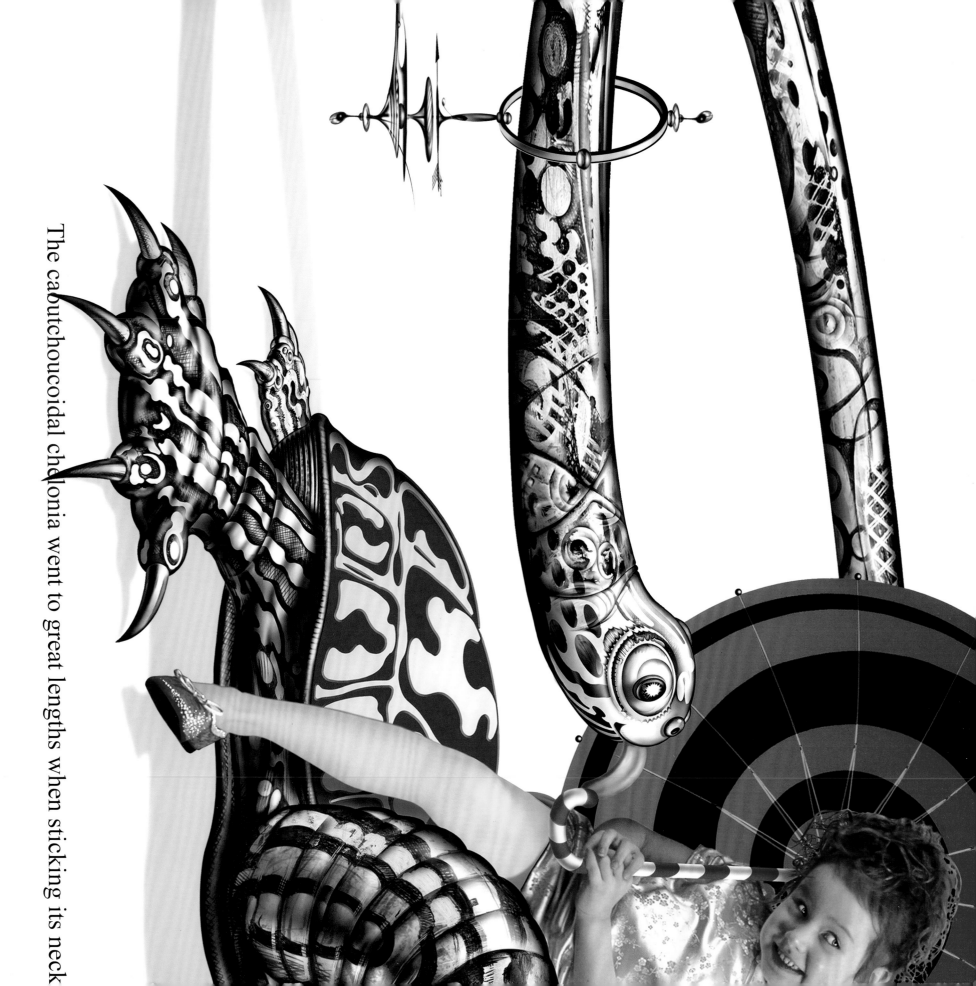

The caoutchoucoidal chelonia went to great lengths when sticking its neck

noodles eating poodles.

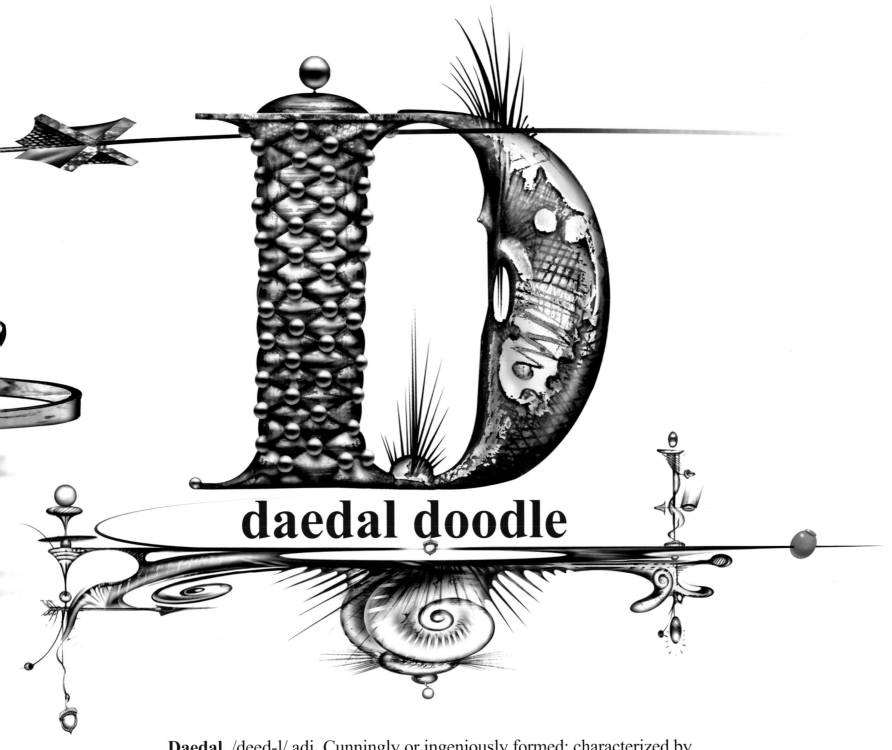

daedal doodle

**Daedal**, /deed-l/ adj. Cunningly or ingeniously formed; characterized by skillful workmanship.
**Doodle**, /dood-l/ vi. Draw aimlessly.

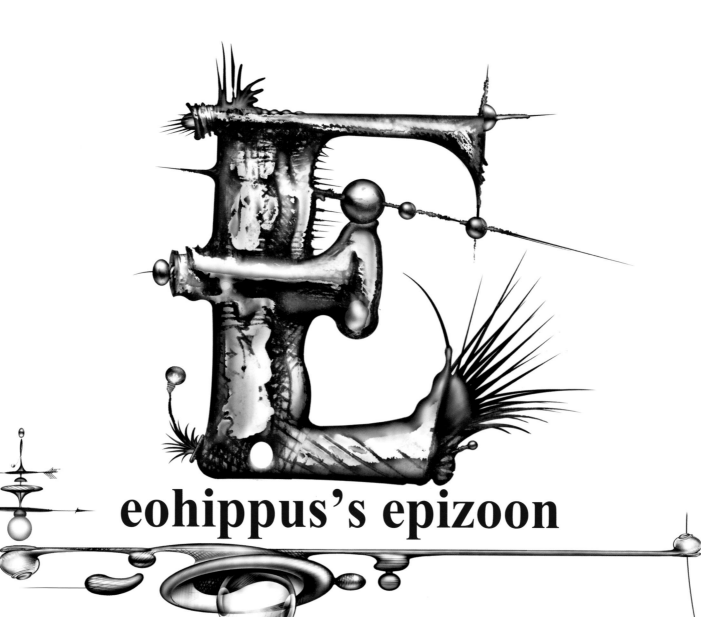

# eohippus's epizoon

**Eohippus**, /ee-oh-hip-uh s/ n. The oldest known horse-like animal.
**Epizoon**, /ep-uh-zoh-on/ n. An animal that lives on the surface of
another animal, whether parasitically or commensally.

Commensally, /kuh-men-suh l/ adv. Characterized by eating
at the same table or living together for mutual benefit.

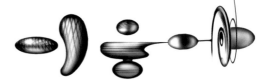

Sadly, the eohippus's epizoon's relationship did not stand the test of time.

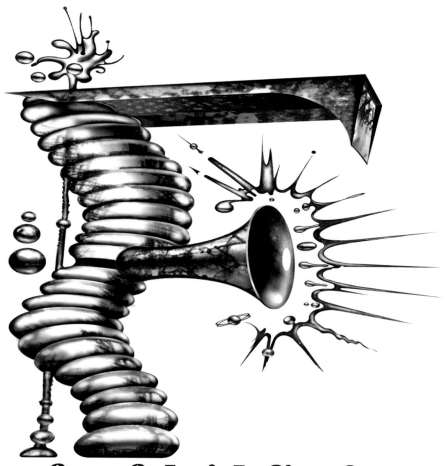

# fanfare for feloid fig faun

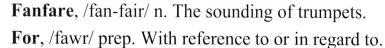

**Fanfare**, /fan-fair/ n. The sounding of trumpets.

**For**, /fawr/ prep. With reference to or in regard to.

**Feloid**, /fee-loid/ adj. Having the characteristics of the cat family.

**Fig faun**, /fig/ /fawn/ n. A mythical creature, represented as living in desert places and eating figs.

The fanfare for feloid fig faun was the official music of the Desert Cat Fig Parade.

# ganoid gubbins

**Ganoid**, /gan-oid/ adj. Of or pertaining to a subclass of fish covered with polished boney plates of scales.
**Gubbins**, /guhb-bins/ n. A device, gizmo or gadget; something unspecified whose name is either forgotten or not known.

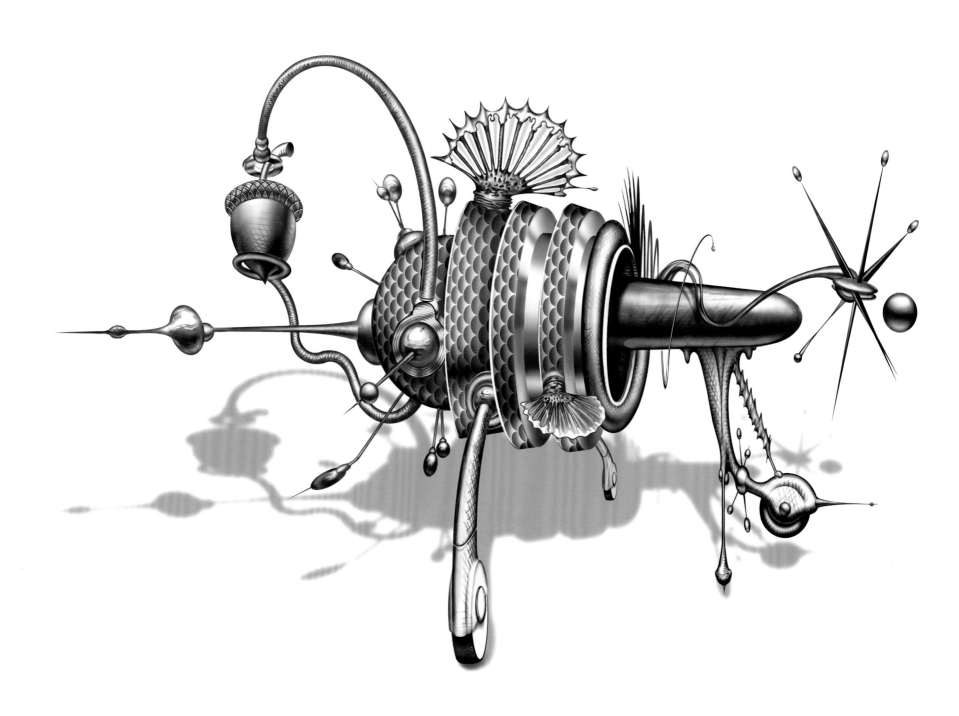

Before being used as a thing-a-ma-jig, the ganoid gubbins was thought to be just another one of those submersible nutcrackers.

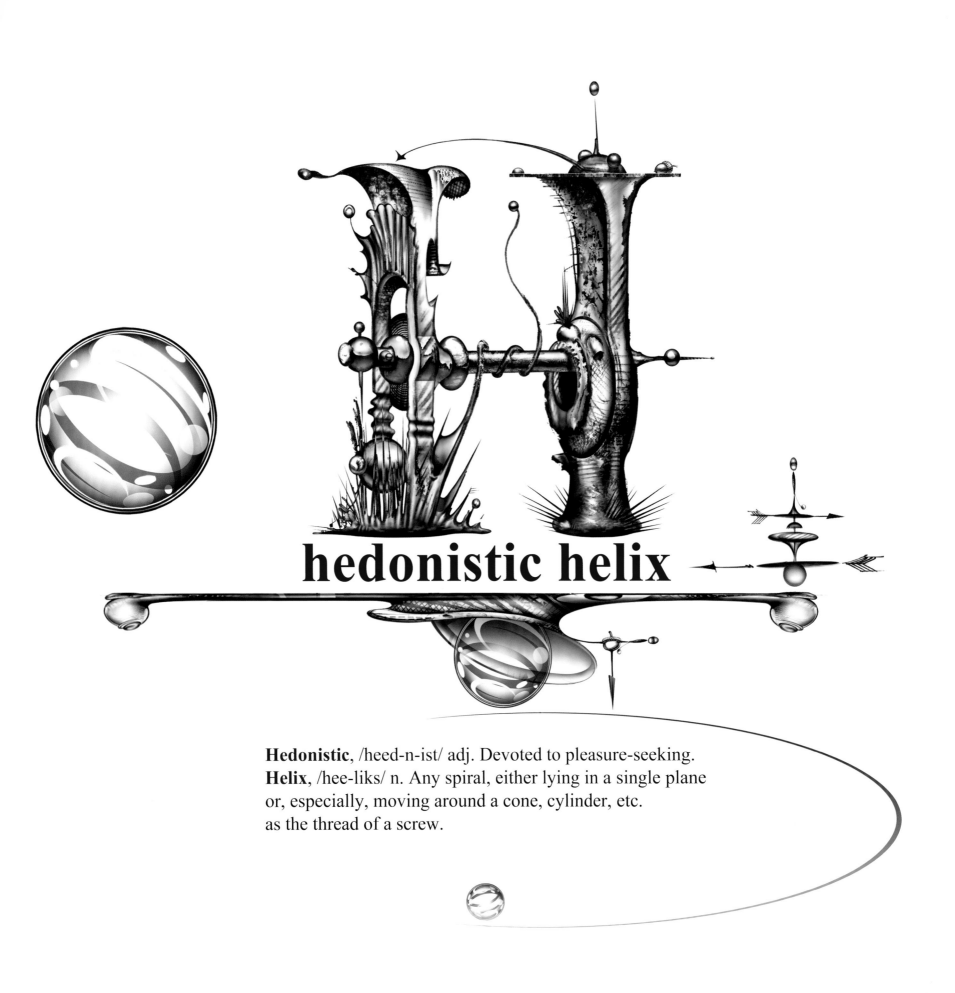

# hedonistic helix

**Hedonistic**, /heed-n-ist/ adj. Devoted to pleasure-seeking.
**Helix**, /hee-liks/ n. Any spiral, either lying in a single plane
or, especially, moving around a cone, cylinder, etc.
as the thread of a screw.

Skyler and Arielle start their bubblicious slide through the circle of life on the hedonistic helix.

# inamorato inamorata

**Inamorato**, /in-am-uh-rah-toh/ n. A man loved; a woman's lover.
**Inamorata**, /in-am-uh-rah-tuh/ n. A woman loved; a man's lover.

My name is inamorato inamorata and I am addicted to love.

# Jansky's jambalaya

**Jansky, Karl Guthe**. 1905-50 engineer, a pioneer in radioastronomy.
**Jansky**, /jan-skee/ n. A unit of flux density for electromagnetic
radiation, used chiefly in radio astronomy.
**Jambalaya**, /juhm-buh-lahy-uh/ n. A dish of Creole origin,
consisting of rice cooked with ham, sausage, chicken, or
shellfish, herbs, spices, and vegetables.

Two out of three astronomers prefer Jansky's jambalaya to green cheese.  Not Bad!

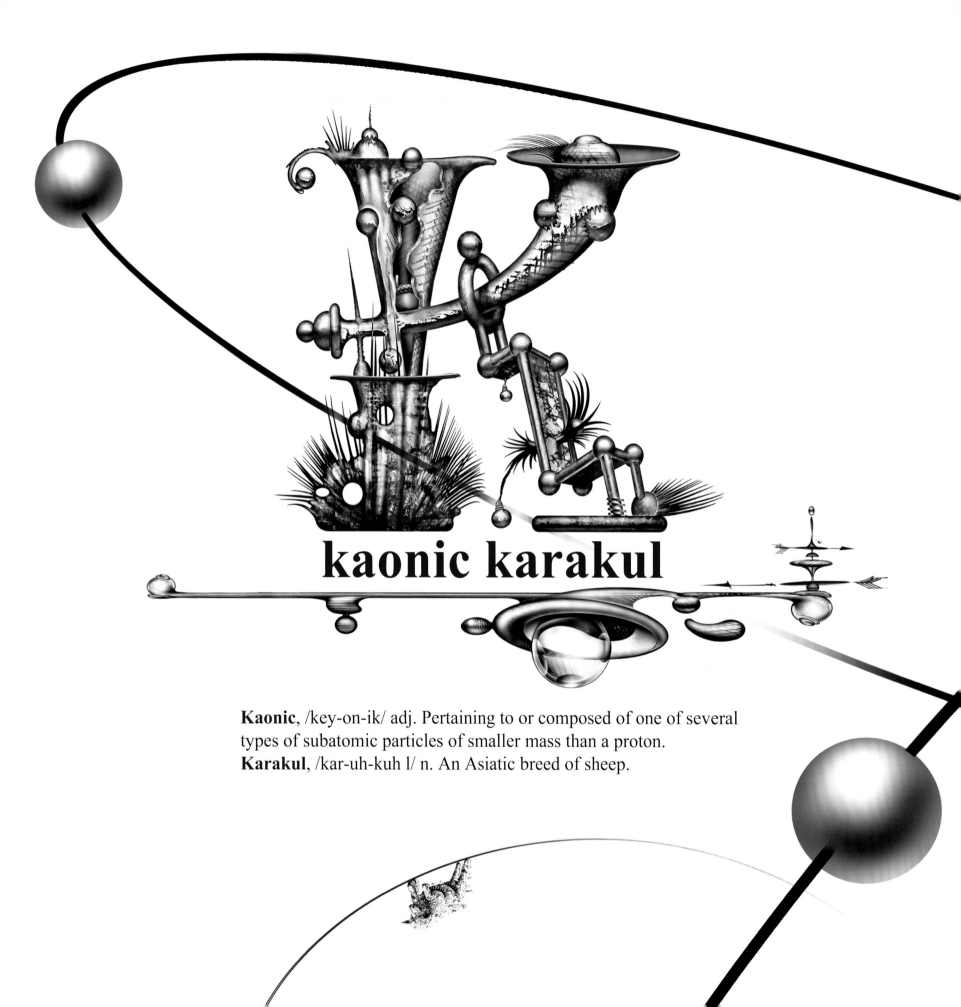

# kaonic karakul

**Kaonic**, /key-on-ik/ adj. Pertaining to or composed of one of several types of subatomic particles of smaller mass than a proton.
**Karakul**, /kar-uh-kuh l/ n. An Asiatic breed of sheep.

Kaonic karakuls are the subatomic sheep that physicists count to go to sleep.

# lissome logophile loach

**Lissome**, /lis-uh m/ adj. Lithe, nimble, flexible.
**Logophile**, /law-guh-fahyl, log-uh-/ n. A lover of words.
**Loach**, /lohch/ n. A small river fish of a family related to carp,
having a long, narrow body and spines around its mouth.

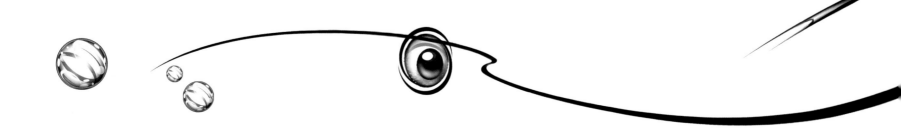

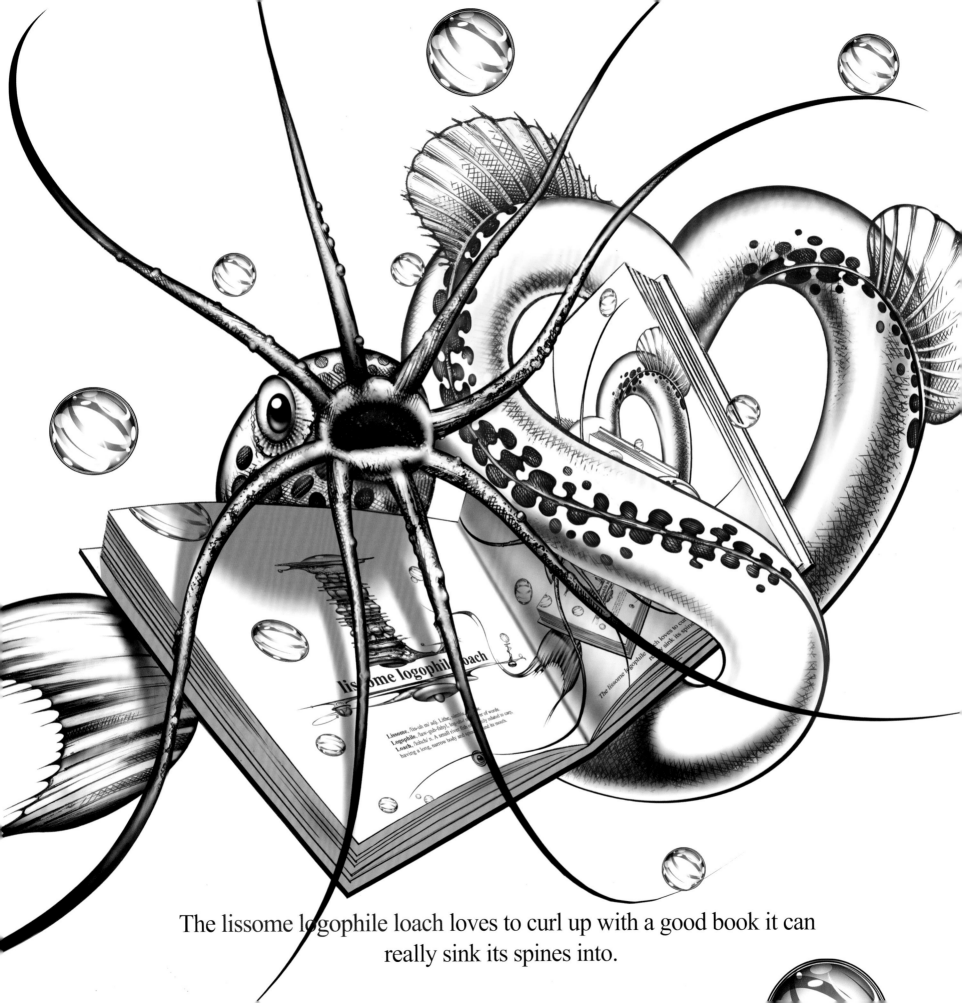

The lissome logophile loach loves to curl up with a good book it can really sink its spines into.

# microcephalic minotaur

**Microcephalic**, /mahy-kroh-suh-fal-ik/ adj. Abnormally small-headed.
**Minotaur**, /min-uh-tawr/ n. Bullheaded monster in the Cretan Labyrinth.

Cretan Labyrinth, /kreet-n/ /lab-uh-rinth/ n. A maze consisting
of a single path winding back and forth to a center point in a
series of seven concentric rings (Google it). It was designed
and constructed by the inventor Daedalus to confine
the Minotaur.

The microcephalic minotaur had more heart than smart.

# nidus naga's nucivorous nidicolous

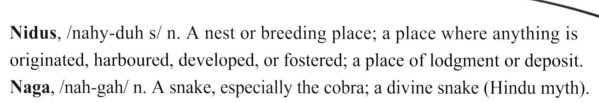

**Nidus**, /nahy-duh s/ n. A nest or breeding place; a place where anything is originated, harboured, developed, or fostered; a place of lodgment or deposit.

**Naga**, /nah-gah/ n. A snake, especially the cobra; a divine snake (Hindu myth).

**Nucivorous**, /noo-siv-er-uh s/ adj. Nut-bearing.

**Nidicolous**, /nahy-dik-uh-luh s/ adj. (Of young birds) staying long in the nest.

**Enigmatically**, /en-ig-mat-ik-ali/ adj. Difficult to interpret or understand; mysterious.

The nidus naga's nucivorous nidicolous had an enigmatically homey
and nuttily long relationship.

# osmotic osprey

**Osmotic**, /oz-moh-sis, os-/ adj. Pertaining to the tendency of a fluid, usually water, to pass through the semipermeable membrane into a solution where the solvent concentration is higher, thus equalizing concentrations of materials on either side of the membrane.

**Osprey**, /os-pree/ n. A large, harmless hawk found worldwide that feeds on fish and builds a bulky nest often occupied for years (tell it to the fish).

**Semipermeable,** /sem-ee-**pur**-mee-*uh-buh* l/ adj. Allowing passage of certain, especially small, molecules or ions but acting as a barrier to others.

swiss cheesesque artist rendering
of a semipermeable membrane

A fish in a brook took a look at a hook - the fisherman protested, "osmotic osprey,
you semipermeable crook."

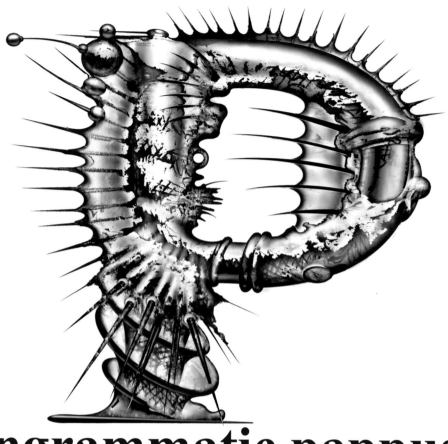

# pangrammatic pappus

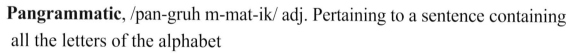

**Pangrammatic**, /pan-gruh m-mat-ik/ adj. Pertaining to a sentence containing all the letters of the alphabet

**Pappus**, /pap-uh s/ n. A ring or parachute of fine hair or down which grows above the seed and helps to disseminate composites and some other plants, e.g., dandelions, by means of wind.

The pangrammatic pappus got off with a light sentence.

# quodlibetical quahog

**Quodlibetical**, /kwod-luh-bet-tik-al/ adj. Not confined to a particular subject; discussed at pleasure for curiosity or entertainment.
**Quahog**, /kwuh-hawg, -hog/ n. A large species of clam.

With nary a care, quodlibetical quahogs go on the air, engaging anything from everywhere and everything from anywhere.

# riparian rill revue

**Riparian**, /ri-pair-ee-uh n, rahy-/ adj. Of or inhabiting a riverbank. n. An owner of land bordering a river.
**Rill**, /ril/ n. A very small brook; a runnel; a small trench; a narrow trench on the moon or Mars.
**Revue**, /ri-vyoo/ n. A loosely constructed theatrical show.

**Runnel**, /ruhn-l/ n. A narrow channel in the ground for liquid to flow through.

From A to Z, water lovers always agree,
the riparian rill revue is the place to be.

# seraphim's simulacrum

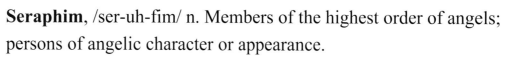

**Seraphim**, /ser-uh-fim/ n. Members of the highest order of angels; persons of angelic character or appearance.
**Simulacrum**, /sim-yuh-ley-kruh m/ n. An unreal or counterfeit resemblance.

The seraphim's simulacrum was angelically drawn and devilishly deceptive.

# tegulated tapir's transvolation

**Tegulated**, /teg-uh-leyt-ed/ adj. Composed of plates overlapping like tiles.
**Tapir**, /tey-per, tuh-peer/ n. A large odd-toed ungulate, eating at night, with a
long flexible proboscis. Several species are found in South America, Malaysia, etc.
**Transvolation**, /trans-voh-luh-shuh n/ n. The act of flying beyond ordinary limits.
**Ungulate**, /uhng-gyuh-lit, -leyt/ n. A mammal having hoofs.

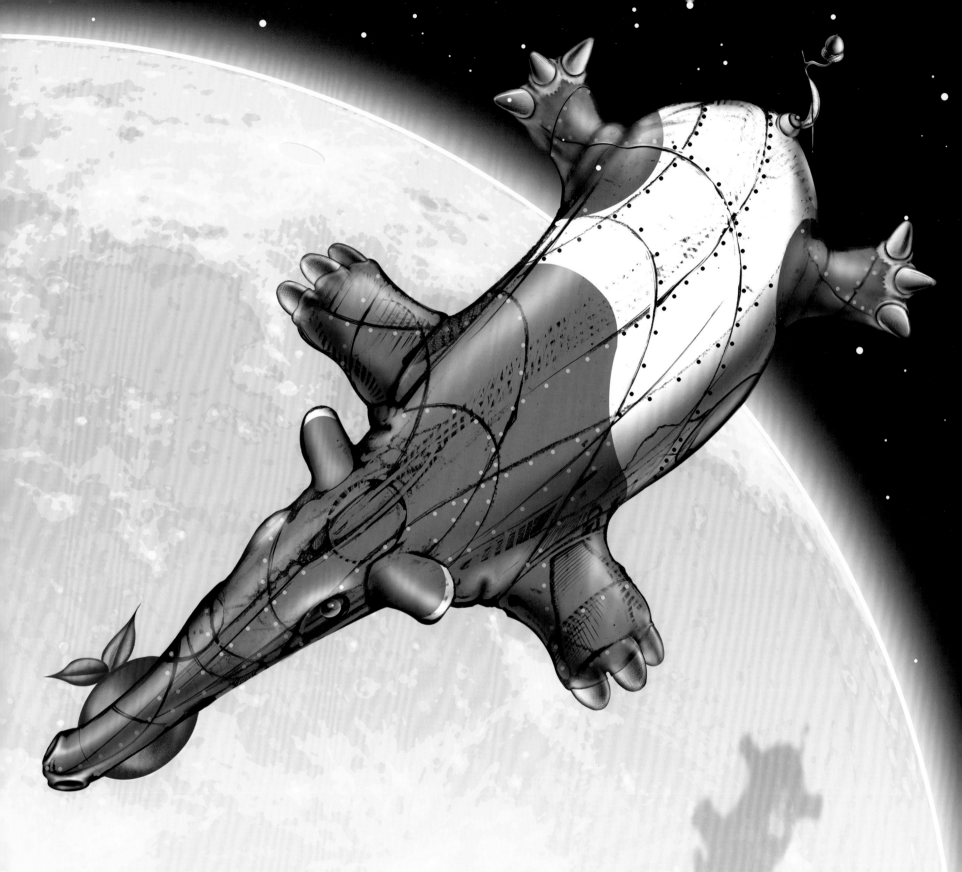

No matter how far the tegulated tapir's transvolation overshot its mark, its ingrained
sense of longitude and latitude always got him home in time for his
evening mud bath and subsequent hoof cleaning.

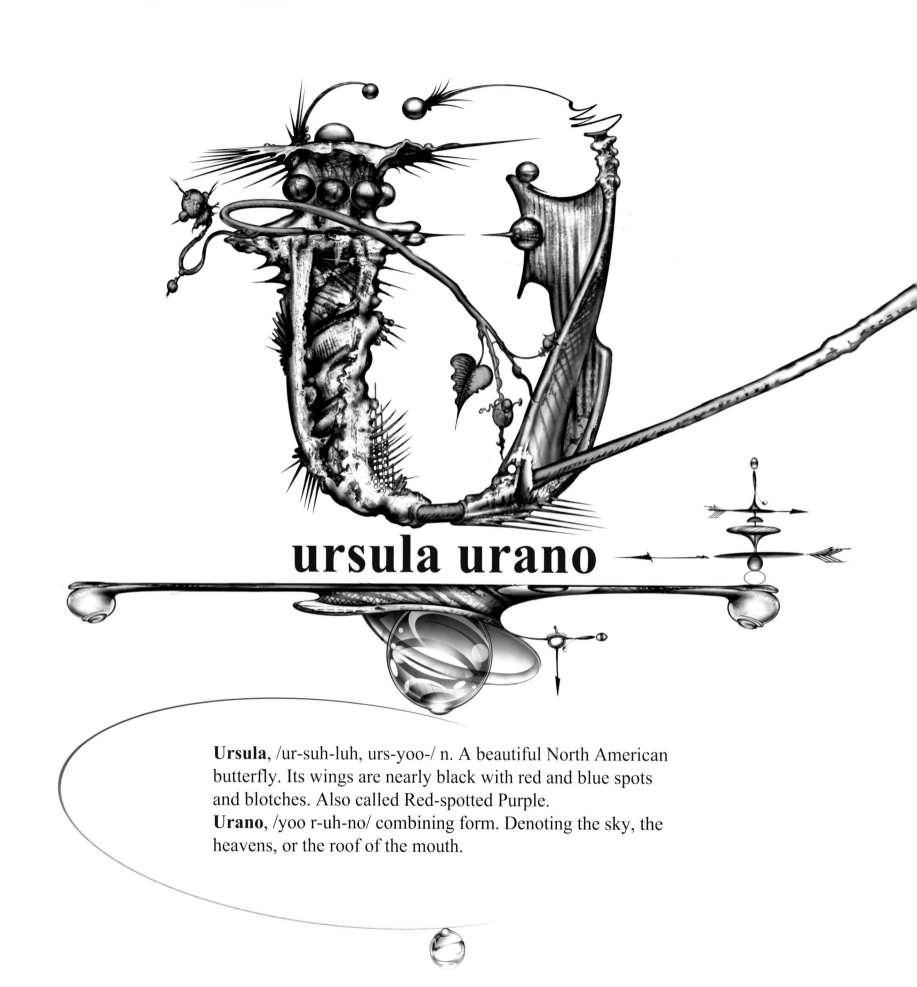

# ursula urano

**Ursula**, /ur-suh-luh, urs-yoo-/ n. A beautiful North American butterfly. Its wings are nearly black with red and blue spots and blotches. Also called Red-spotted Purple.

**Urano**, /yoo r-uh-no/ combining form. Denoting the sky, the heavens, or the roof of the mouth.

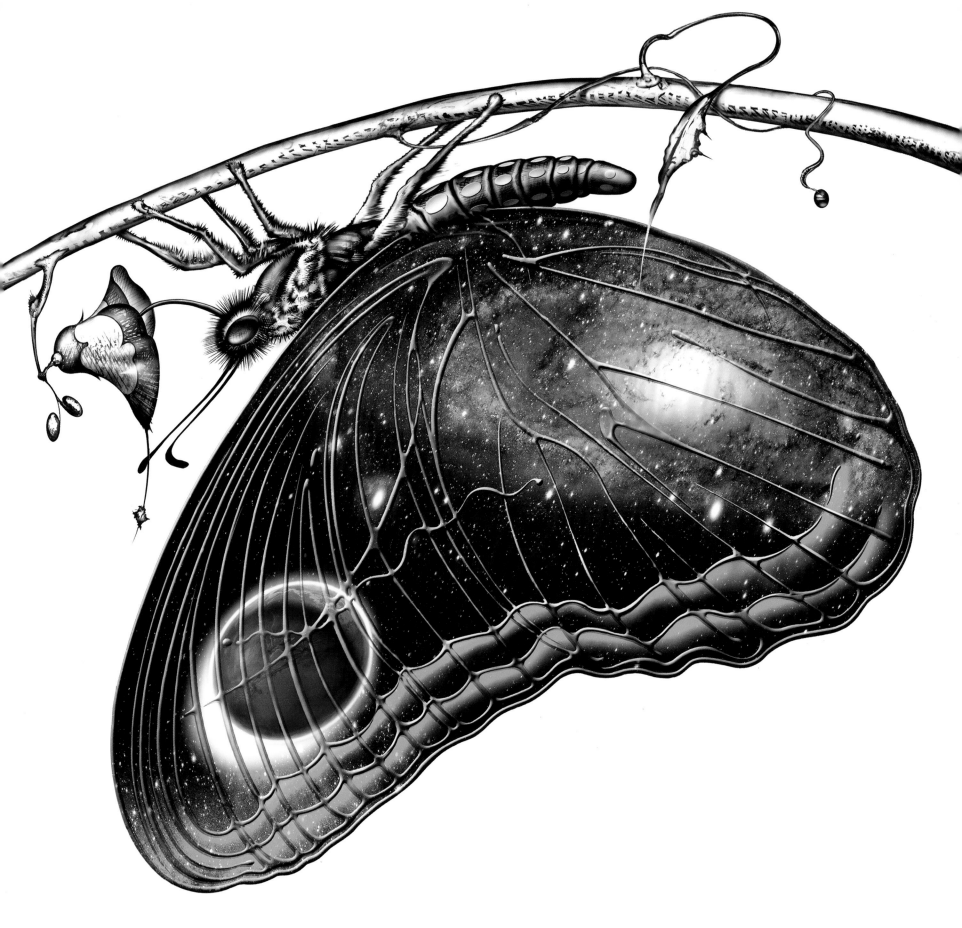

And on the 8th day the ursula urano pollinated the universe.

**Verso** n. A left-hand page of an open book; the reverse of a coin or metal.

When not on the fly, the vedalia's vaccary voluted vade-mecum read books
in reverse to groovy twisted house-bound cows.

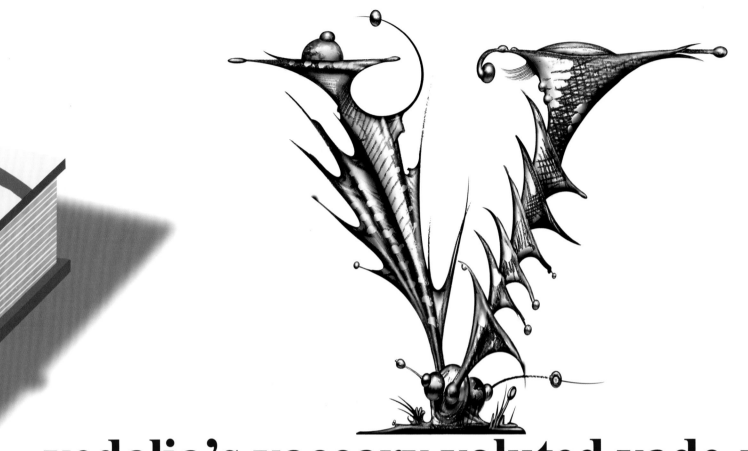

# vedalia's vaccary voluted vade-mecum

**Vedalia**, /vi-dey-lee-uh/ n. Australian ladybug.
**Vaccary**, /vak-ka-ree/ n. A cow house.
**Voluted**, /vuh-loot-ed/ adj. Grooved or twisted in spirals.
**Vade-mecum**, /vey-dee/ /mee-kuh m/ n. [Latin "go with me"]
A handbook or pocket-companion.

# woubit whigmaleerie

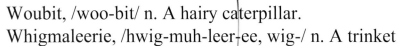

Woubit, /woo-bit/ n. A hairy caterpillar.
Whigmaleerie, /hwig-muh-leer-ee, wig-/ n. A trinket
or knickknack; a fantastic ornamentation; a whim.

Before getting its Christmas coiffure, the woubit whigmaleerie looked like two of the Beatles.

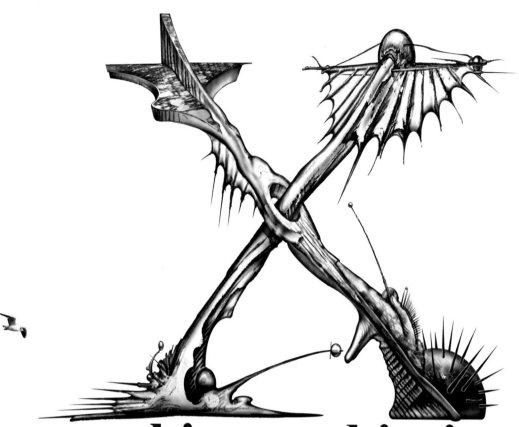

# xenomorphic xenobiosis xenium

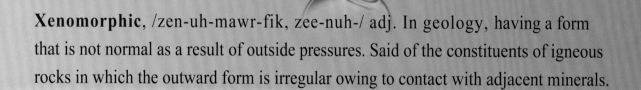

**Xenomorphic**, /zen-uh-mawr-fik, zee-nuh-/ adj. In geology, having a form that is not normal as a result of outside pressures. Said of the constituents of igneous rocks in which the outward form is irregular owing to contact with adjacent minerals.

**Xenobiosis**, /zen-uh-bahy-oh-sis/ n. A form of communal life in which two colonies of different species live together on friendly terms, but do not rear their young in common.

**Xenium**, /ze-nee-uh m/ n. A gift to a guest.

The secret formula for making xenomorphic xenobiosis xenium key lime gift pie
is knowing when to say goodnight.

# yava-skin ypsiliform ylem

**Yava-skin**, /yah-vuh skin/ n. A kind of Elephantiasis caused by the habitual use of Kava.

**Ypsiliform**, /ip-sil-i-fawrm/ adj. Y-shaped.

**Ylem**, /ahy-luh m/ n. In cosmology the original matter that existed before the formation of chemical elements, pre-Big Bang matter.

**Kava**, /kah-vuh/ n. A Polynesian shrub, of the pepper family, the aromatic roots of which are used to make an intoxicating beverage.

Hi Andy!

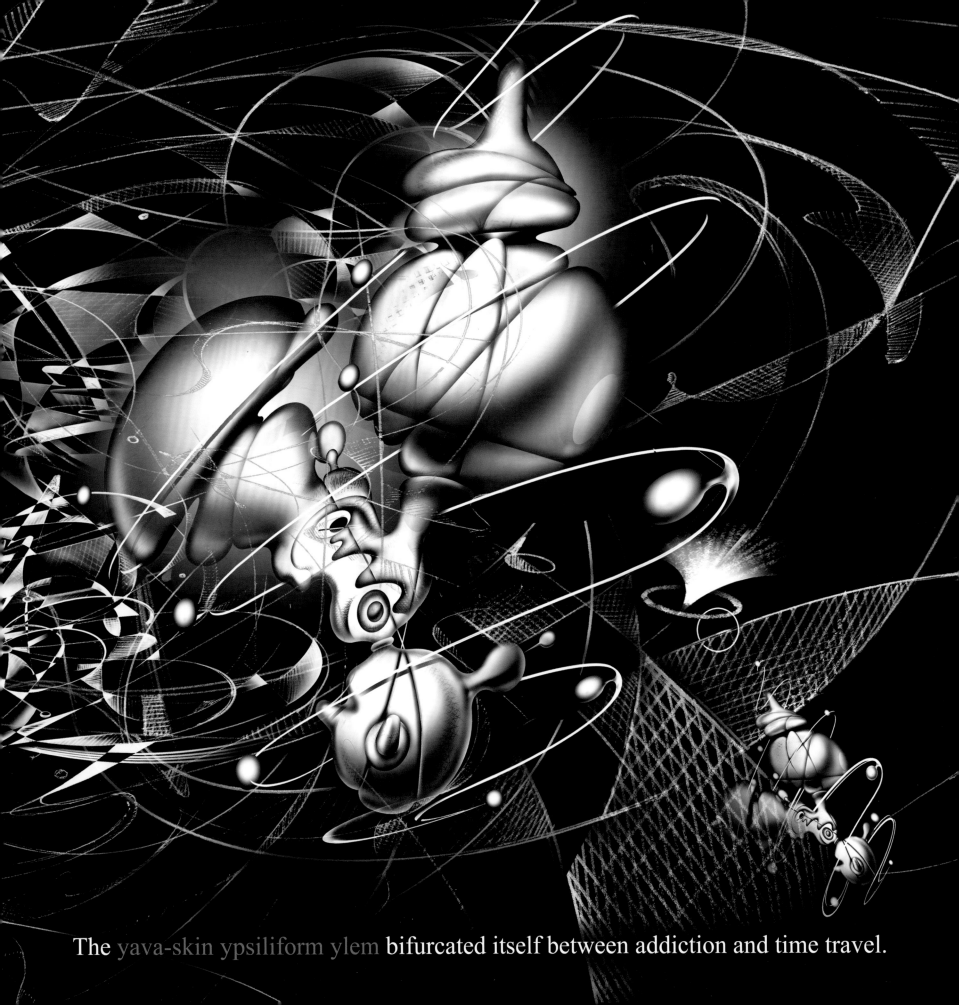

The yava-skin ypsiliform ylem bifurcated itself between addiction and time travel.

# zooid zeppelin's zygote

**Zooid**, /zoh-oid/ n. An organic body or cell having locomotion, as a spermatic cell.

**Zeppelin**, /zep-uh-lin/ n. A dirigible, cigar-shaped airship of the type designed by Count Zeppelin (c. 1900).

**Zygote**, /zahy-goht, zig-oht/ n. The product of the union of two gametes; by extension, the individual developing from that product.

**Gamete**, /gam-eet, guh-meet/ n. A sexual reproduction cell; an egg cell or sperm cell.

The zooid zeppelin's zygote's independent travels led to the conception of floating cigar shaped flight.

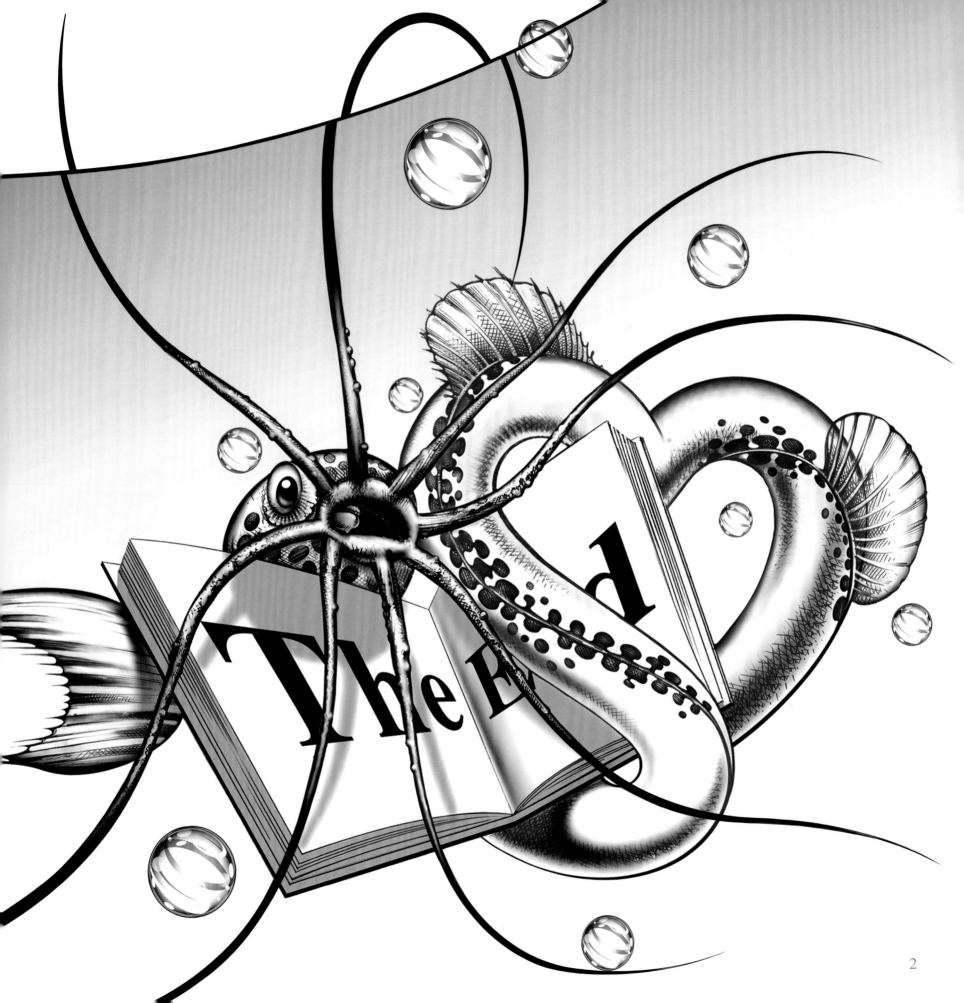

**Addenda,** *plural noun*. Items of additional material, added at the end of a book or other publication.

### Are the words in the alliterations real?

*Yes. In fact, Victor spent countless hours sifting
through thousands of pages of dictionaries to find them.*

### What is the logic behind the sentences?

*As improbable as it might seem, the poetic wordplay in the text reveals the meanings
of the featured alliterations. They're all designed to make you think. Some of
the sentences might make you laugh. Some may even do both.*

### Why are some definitions in *blue?*

*These are bonus words: Words found inside the
definitions of the alliterations and sentences; words too
compelling and useful to ignore.*

### What's up with the acorns?

*Read "Dictionary as Muse" in the front of the book and find out.*

### Are you answering these questions truthfully?

*Open a dictionary and see for yourself.*

### Have Victor Stabin and the Microcephalic Minotaur ever been seen at the same time in the same place?

*Visit* www.victorstabin.com *and find out.*

# An Afternoon at the Museum

## notations on a theme

The education department at the Metropolitan Museum of Art invited me to teach a class based on the making of Daedal Doodle. To come up with alliterations such as Appreceptive Achatina, Bifoliated Bonito and Caoutchouidal Chelonia, I read 8,000 pages in various dictionaries. But for this class, in addition to using the dictionary as a word source, we also used the Museum's Oceania Galleries where the museum displays artifacts from the peoples of Polynesia, New Britain, Australia and New Guinea.

The class consisted of students between 9 and 18 year olds. Before giving an assignment to a such a young group, I created a sample image to let the class better understand what they were being asked to do. Initially, I did the assignment out of a sense of responsibility. However, after roaming the Met's galleries, the assignment blossomed into a world of unimagined possibilities that reminded me why I created Daedal Doodle in the first place. I was stunned by the looney*, otherworldly Kavat Masks of the Baining people. I had never come across something so physically and culturally ornate, or so spiritually enchanting.

The next part of the assignment was to go to the letter "K" section of the dictionary and find a word or words that would complete the alliteration. Sometimes finding the right word takes a while. This time it happened in minutes. I found the word Khedah. My imagination felt like comets colliding in space. I immediately changed the scale of the Kavat to be the walls of the **Khedah** thereby creating the ...

### KAVATESQUE KHEDAH

Tah-Da

*Looney is not meant as a pejorative but rather is an example of my initial ignorance of the Baining / New Guinean culture. With a little investigation it became apparent that their beliefs are ecologically vibrant and are as anthropologically exciting as the thought of visiting another planet.

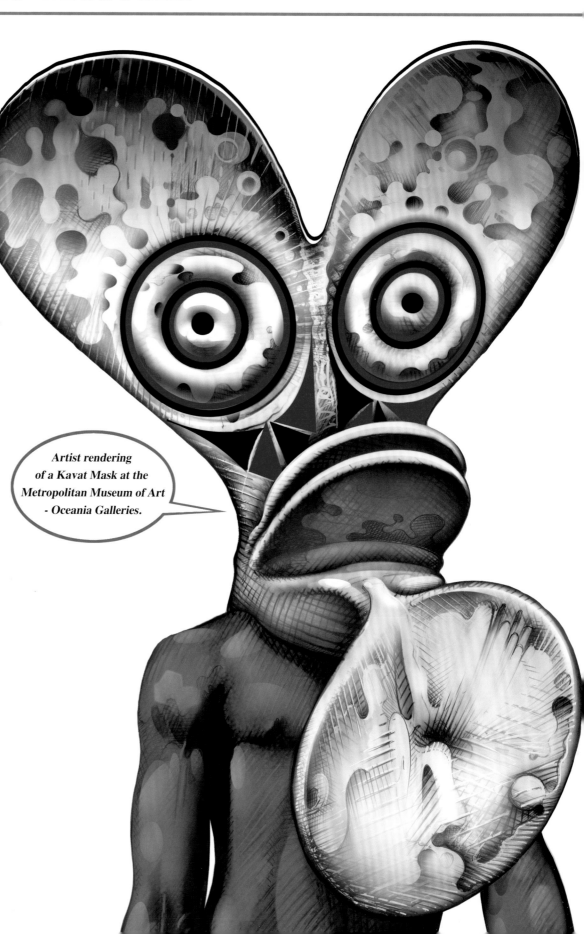

*Artist rendering of a Kavat Mask at the Metropolitan Museum of Art - Oceania Galleries.*

**Kavat,** *n*. The dramatic bark cloth kavat masks created by New Guinean's Central Baining people, are used exclusively in night dance. These masks represent spirits associated with the forks of tree trunks.

**Khedah,** *n*. (in India, Myanmar, etc) an enclosure into which wild elephants are driven to be captured.

# ictionary as Curriculum

Daedal Doodle was created using the dictionary as a map. From it, I learned the power of a single word to create images.

Over a three-and-a-half-year period I culled lists of descriptive words previously unknown or unused by me, doing it one letter section at a time. My sources were a 2,000-page Merriam Webster's Dictionary that my dad had brought home when I was four, the Oxford English Dictionary that I bought for my dad when I was 30, and the Chambers Concise Dictionary—my favorite—a dictionary published in Scotland. I read and reread the lists as I compiled them. The process created the alliterations that seemed to magically transform themselves into images.

I had no idea that my book's first stop would be at Panther Valley High School—a school 10 miles from my home in Jim Thorpe, PA. It was the quintessential "There's no place like home" moment. Seemingly out of the blue, I became part of the Allentown Art Museum's Artist in Residence program, funded by the Pennsylvania Council of the Arts and the National Endowment for the Arts.

I presented my work to the student body in the high school auditorium, showing my "Turtle Series" paintings, Daedal Doodle and highlights from my 25-year career as an illustrator. Serendipitously, 26 kids chose to take my class. I knew I wanted these students to make their own version of my ABC book.

The lesson plan mimicked the process I went through to create Daedal Doodle. First, I assigned each student a letter of the alphabet. They had to make lists with brief definitions of "new words," unfamiliar nouns and adjectives, and even the occasional verb. I told them to seek out words that had a "bounce," words that sounded cool, words that provoked imagery.

Though the words appeared to be random, I believe they were personal in nature, selected because there was some sort of connection to the reader's life experiences. Since the project started in an art course, my job was to demonstrate a process that could easily be understood, that would encourage students to come up with something completely new to them, something that they could call "Art." The kids were open to what looked more like fun than work.

Sitting in a room full of students simultaneously reading the dictionary was my "Aha!" moment.

The success of this "Dictionary Curriculum" reminds me of the serendipitous invention of Teflon. Apparently, there was some odorless substance - a strange byproduct of the previous experiment - at the bottom of a beaker that could not be washed, burnt, or chemically dissolved away. After examination by Roy J. Plunkett, a young chemist, Teflon went on to become a gigantic industry for decades. Plunkett often told student audiences that his mind was prepared by education and training to "recognize novelty."

Reading a dictionary to source words that inspire drawings is a novel way to bridge art and language. It could easily help put an end to the traditionally rigid separation of the arts from basic education.

At Panther Valley High, each student proudly came up with some brilliantly alliterative pictorial word invention. Their only tools were a dictionary, a pencil and paper. The byproduct was an appreciation for the dictionary, a new way to visually conceptualize, an enthusiasm for drawing and the self esteem that follows creative work and expanding one's vocabulary.

People often ask me where I received my art training. Although I attended The Los Angeles Art Center College of Design and The School of Visual Arts, I usually say that I got my start at New York City's High School of Art & Design. Forty years after graduating I went back to A&D and showed my work to its senior class. I was then invited to exhibit my work in their main gallery and give the keynote speech to the graduating class.

At the ceremony, I noted that A&D alumnus, Art Spiegelman, the creator of the graphic novel Maus, established an award for the best cartooning graduate called, "The Maus Award." This inspired me to create an award for best creative drawing called the "Daedal Doodle Award." The school asked me to base the award on a contest and pick the winner.

Again, I had the kids make an ABC book using the Daedal Doodle process. This time, I directed them to use the Museum of Natural History's extinct species section for their initial reference and to complete the alliteration by using a dictionary. This class was fortunate to have the painter, James Harrington, as their instructor. The students all came up with terrific alliterations, and the students with the best drawing and ideas won. The work was so consistently eye popping that I decided to split the award four ways - which was still hard to do considering the high quality of the class's work.

Presented on the opposite page,
the High School of Art & Design 2014 Senior Illustration Class - *The Daedal Doodle Award for Conceptual Drawing* - winners.

## Belligerent Bifurcated Bovid
### Diana Vidal

*The **Belligerent Bifurcated Bovid** was feeling rather cut up after his fight.*

**Belligerent**, adj. aggressive or hostile - **Bifurcated**, v. divided in two parts
**Bovid**, n.  A hoofed, dual horned mammal.

## Ludic Lepus curpaeums
### Clare Cho

*The enthusiastic **Ludic Lepus curpaeums** bursted into an asymmetric elliptical frenzy.*

**Ludic**, adj. Showing spontaneous and undirected playfulness.
**Lepus curpaeums**, n. A wild hare.

## Yagi Yaveh
### Melissa Guachun

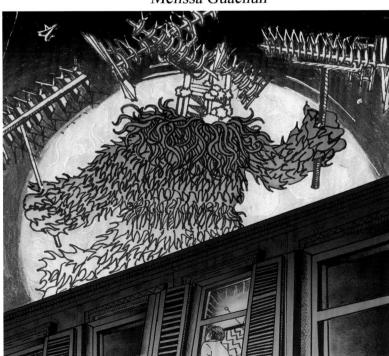

*The **Yagi Yaveh** rooftop reception was more startling than directional.*

**Yagi,** n. A directional radio and television antenna consisting of a horizontal conductor with several insulated dipoles. - **Yaveh**, n. An African costume used for portraying evil.

## Scopophobic Stenomylus-hitchcocki
### Hazien Lyles-Saunders

*For the **Scopophobic Stenomylus-hitchcocki** getting from point A to point B felt like walking through hallways of eyeballs.*

**Scopophobic** n.  Extreme or irrational fear of being looked at or seen.
**Stenomylus hitchcocki** n.  A Gazell-Camel last seen in Nebraska's Agate Fossil Beds.

# radio stories
## unauthorized cautionary tales

What happens when hybrid creatures living in surreal environments go through their daily routines with the radio on?

While working on Daedal Doodle I was repeatedly asked, "What are these characters' stories?"

I was trained from birth to listen to talk radio. As a kid, I grew up listening to New York's WOR, WINS and WNYC. As an adult, I never strayed far from WNYC (which is my browser home page) or National Public Radio. I didn't want to write a book of stories as much as I wanted to get back to painting, but the repeated nagging question never stopped:

"What are these characters' stories?"

I began to write stories about these unusual characters, weaving my love of listening to National Public Radio into each tale. The series *Radio Stories* was born.

Daedal Doodle's Letter Q is the Quodlibetical Quahog, a giant NPR broadcasting clam that takes pleasure talking about anything and everything. In these stories, Daedal Doodle's characters go through their daily routines while listening to the NPR broadcasting clam read the news, do interviews and make commentary

For Example:

Letter A: The Apperceptive Achatina - After hearing about what's happening to frogs, this self reflective Giant African Snail ponders his demise while gazing at his image in the toaster.

Letter B: The Bifoliated Bonito - A mackerel that's part fish and part plant finds out he's swimming in a pharmaceutical cocktail of Prozac, Lipitor, Ambien and Viagra.

Letter C: The Caoutchoucoidal Chelonia - An extraordinarily long-necked, rubber-bush-eating turtle becomes an NPR commentator and a crusader for oceanic preservation.

I've asked other writers whether they'd be interested in following "the talking clam cautionary tale" format. I've invited them to pick any character from Daedal Doodle and pen their own *Radio Stories* tale (a suggested thousand words in length).

My first few *Radio Stories* have attracted other artists and authors to contribute their own sections, including Andy Lanset, Director of Archives, New York Public Radio; Marshall Arisman, artist/author and MFA Illustration as Visual Essay Department Chair at SVA; Tad Crawford, author of The Secret Life of Money and A Floating Life; Tina Traster, columnist and author of Burb Appeal; and Dr. Carl Safina, noted preservationist and award winning author.

Tips for Writers
If you are interested in contributing to the *Radio Stories* collection, pick a character from Daedal Doodle and tell us your version of what happens - when the character goes through their daily routine with the radio tuned to NPR. Please remember that the radio broadcaster is always a version of the Quodlibetical Quahog (AKA The Chatty Clam), otherwise known as the "Q" character from Daedal Doodle.

*For an example, please note my penning for letter C's story on the following spread.*

Writers are encouraged to follow this format and incorporate NPR's broadcasting style into the stories. The Radio Stories are Cautionary Tales featuring protagonists from Daedal Doodle, inspired by NPR news and information programming, and served with a side of Aesop's Fables. If you're interested in reading more of these stories and possibly penning one of your own go to - radio stories - on the menu bar of my website to find the other stories and up-to-date details.

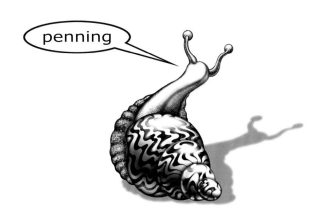

Scott the Quahog Simon

**Caoutchoucoidal**, /kou-chook-oid-uh l/ adj. Made of India rubber, an elastic gum, or the dried juice of one of numerous tropical plants of the dogbane, spurge, and nettle families. Caoutchoucoidal objects are extremely elastic vand impervious to water and to nearly all other fluids.

**Chelonia**, /ke-lo-ni-a/ n. Tortoises and turtles.

# OILS WELL THAT ENDS WELL

## A Chelonian Tale of Swimming in the Gulf of Mexico

It was the longest of necks, it was the shortest of necks. It was the atavistic memory of 220 million years of sub-marinal migration, it was a common elastic subtropical plant, it was all the songs of the sea encoded on delicate strands of DNA. It was snappin' gum to pop tunes on the radio. It was the eternal spring of hope, it was death flirting with the circle of life from the edge of the maelstrom, it was witness to the birth of prehistory, the new world and the next world. It had everything before it and it seemed that, one way or the other, it always would.

Like his ancestors before him, Cao-Che's migratory wanderlust sent him ricocheting around the globe bearing witness to its seemingly never ending magic. His forebearers had seen the invention of the wheel, the Hanging Gardens of Babylon, the discovery of fire, the burning of the Library at Alexandria (that was a real eyebrow raiser) and the birth of Abraham, Muhammad and Jesus. In Cao-Che's lifetime: the internal combustion engine, motor oil, the invention of radio and the end of ship-to-shore semaphore*. All that and more changed the world, but other than the lack of occasional flag waving, Cao-Che's world seemed pretty stable – for the most part.

*Semaphore, n. A system of sending messages by holding the arms or two flags or poles in certain positions according to an alphabetic code.

For the most part - Mother Nature was never an issue a robust turtle couldn't handle - for the most part. Cao-Che was in for a surprise.

For the last two hundred years, his sojourns had been solitary, actually not an uncommon trait in a turtle. But Cao-Che was different. He was only half turtle. The other half was Caoutchouc Bush – and bushes enjoyed being planted next to other like-minded bushes.

Dramatic Pause . . .

Cao-Che attained a graceful balance through constant swimming. He ate an extraordinarily fresh and varied diet, and never thought twice about migrating thousands of miles, following currents and temperatures, depending on the kind of dinner he fancied. Swimming and dining for almost 200 years and barely looking a day over 100. An exemplary Chelonian life – except for one thing. The bush thing. Every now and then he thought about going for a walk, if for no other reason than to just hang out, dry out and stretch out.

From Nova Scotia in November to New Orleans in December. A journey of about 1,400 miles south, a gentle right turn up into the Gulf of Mexico, then due north and west to Louis's land of dreams. Being that it was not the longest of all trips and that Cao-Che had just feasted off the banks of the Northeast, the plan was to wait till N'Orleans before worrying about food.

No matter how free a man dreams he is, he is never as free as a fish.

Drifting on liquid Van Allen Belts through clouds of teeming, streaming life, his 360° vision, from eyes on opposite sides of the head, rendered swimming the dream phantasmagoric, without distinction between the conscious and unconscious, everything is and everything was, except for the smell. Oh, things looked normal. But ... there was this DNA-awakening smell... a smell from the good old days over 66,000,000 years ago, when all there really was to worry about was being bullied back into the water by T Rex & Company.

Against his better judgment, more curious than repelled, he followed what he smelled, and suddenly found himself cloaked in what appeared to be an enormous kaleidoscopic lava lamp made of smiling chocolate jelly fish. As hungry as Cao-Che was from the trip, he knew to stay away. Stay away from the bounty-ounty. Oh no, oh boy, oh my. Oh snap. Smell imbued, Cao-Che started to do a backward Calder-esque sideways dance while eating his way through a universe of shiny, singing, gooey, smiling, parading, escaping, giant black petroleum jelly fish.

WOW

One moment stinky, next moment knocked back. Exit stage left, ass up in the alley, upside-down reptile dysfunction worse than the brown acid at Woodstock. Worse than buying used cars from twin gypsy car dealers, worse than floating in total stasis suffering the indignities of full on sphilkes*-ectomy.

WOW again.

Mobilized with every emergency vehicle available the entire southern coast was ready for the expected shoreline arrivals. Headlines Read: WASHED UP NEAR DEAD! Muscles as loose as a goose with a neck longer than a giraffe. Riding in the presidential ambulance, breathing pure oxygen (at this point dear patient reader the author cannot reiterate enough how thankful he is to have a President that gives a f!@k about fish).

The toxic shock wore off as delirium set in. His retinas, stained with the high-contrast amorphic shapes of the oil blobs that blocked out the sun, were now ghosting the corners of the inside of the mobile emergency room. Cao-Che could hear voices, but nobody's lips were moving. It sounded like a clam having an impromptu interview with an authority on, of all things, turtle mythology.

In fact it was Scott "the Quahog" Simon speaking on NPR's "All Things Quodlibetical"*, discussing the discovery of a new turtle species. NPR's on the scene expert, Dr. Carl Safina was explaining an ancient myth from a lost tribe of India. "Well Scott, to genetically engineer an unusually long necked Chelonia, the tribe fed Caoutchouc nectar to infant turtles. They were a tribe of marine explorers who believed the iconic neck enabled them to see beyond the horizon. Finding this creature, Scott, well it's as significant as finding Atlantis," Safina said.

As the dust settled, Cao-Che became world famous, sought after for his intrepid stories of migration, revered for his wisdom, cherished as a symbol of species diversity and empathized with as a survivor / representative of one of the world's greatest man-made disasters. Cao-Che quickly became the venerable star commentator on "All Things Quodlibetical." No matter where Cao-Che showed up, the spectacle of his appearance brought waves of oceanic stewardship, widening man's concern for life past the shoreline. Because of neck modesty, radio became Cao-Che's medium of choice. He had a neck for radio.

Cao-Che became the symbol for responsible energy, and singlehandedly ended off-shore oil drilling. Today, in his spare time, when he's not balancing the weight of the world, Cao-Che loves to hang out with children, loves to chew extremely sugary gum and really goes crazy when he hears *The Turtles* on the radio.

*Sphilkes, v. Ants in ones pants.
*page Q

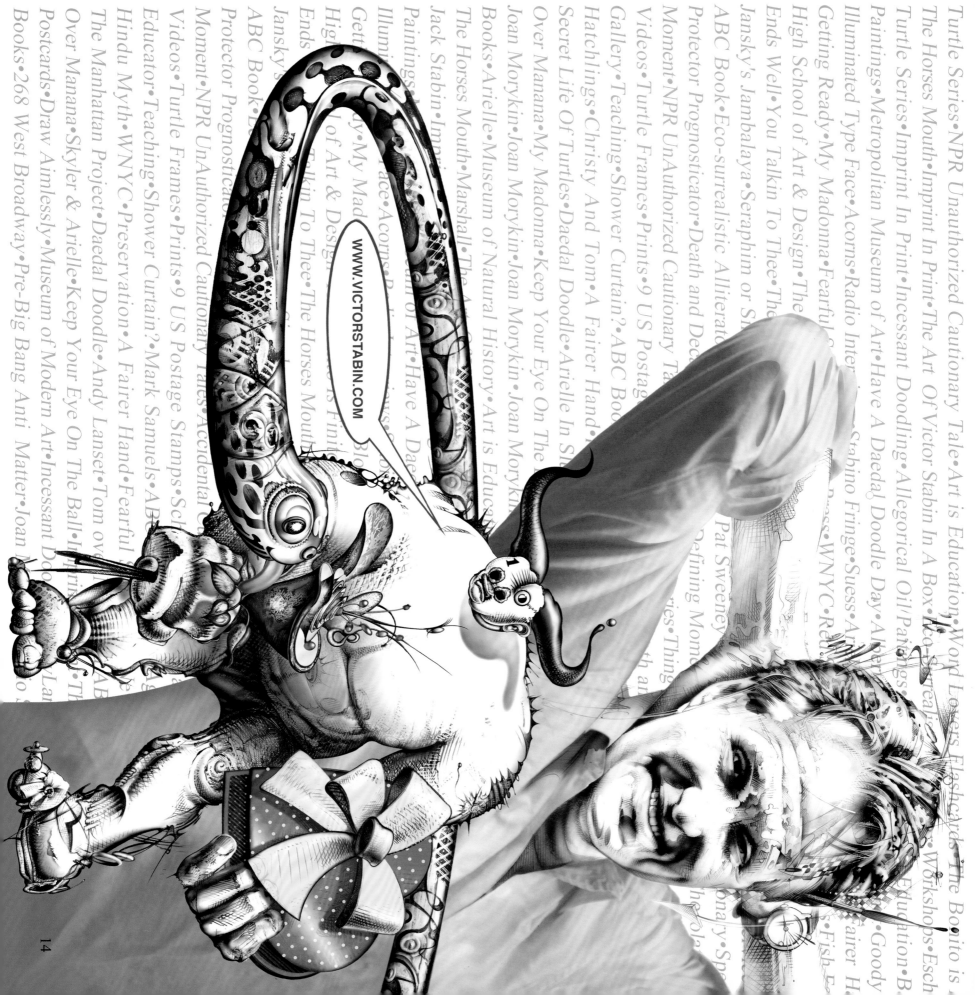

WWW.VICTORSTABIN.COM

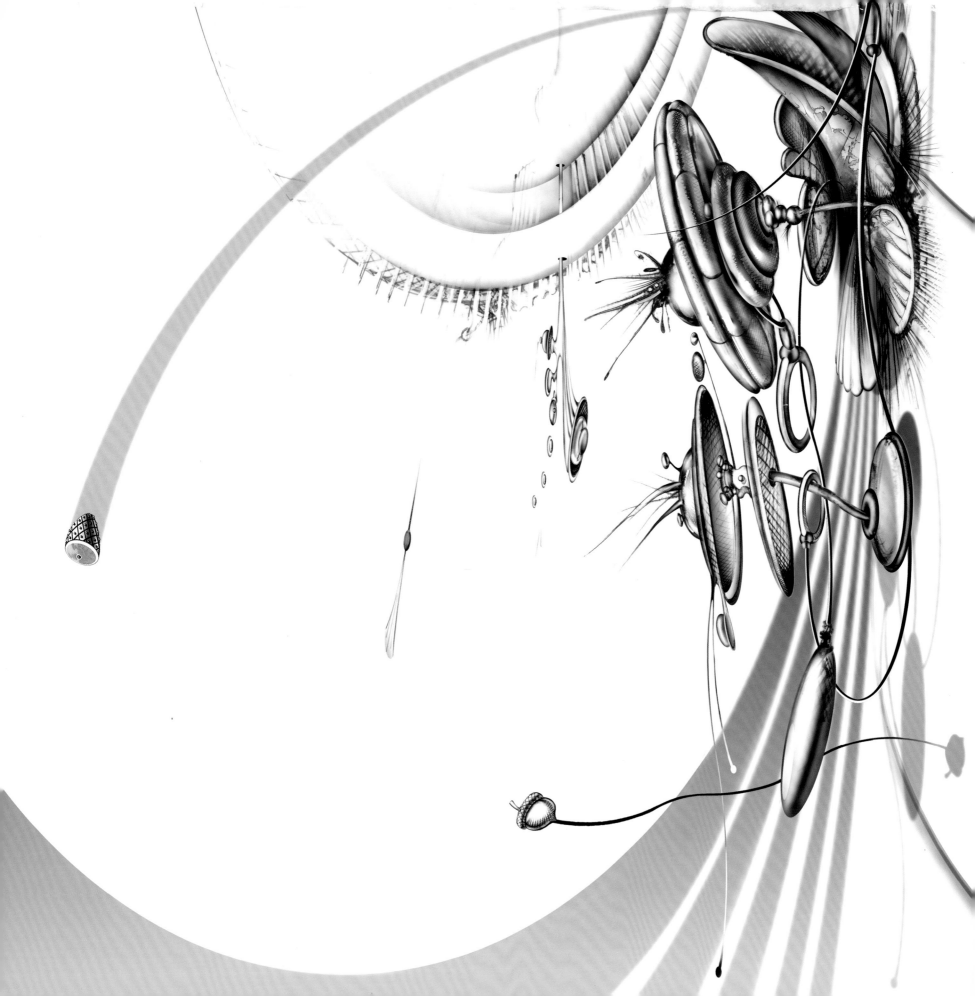

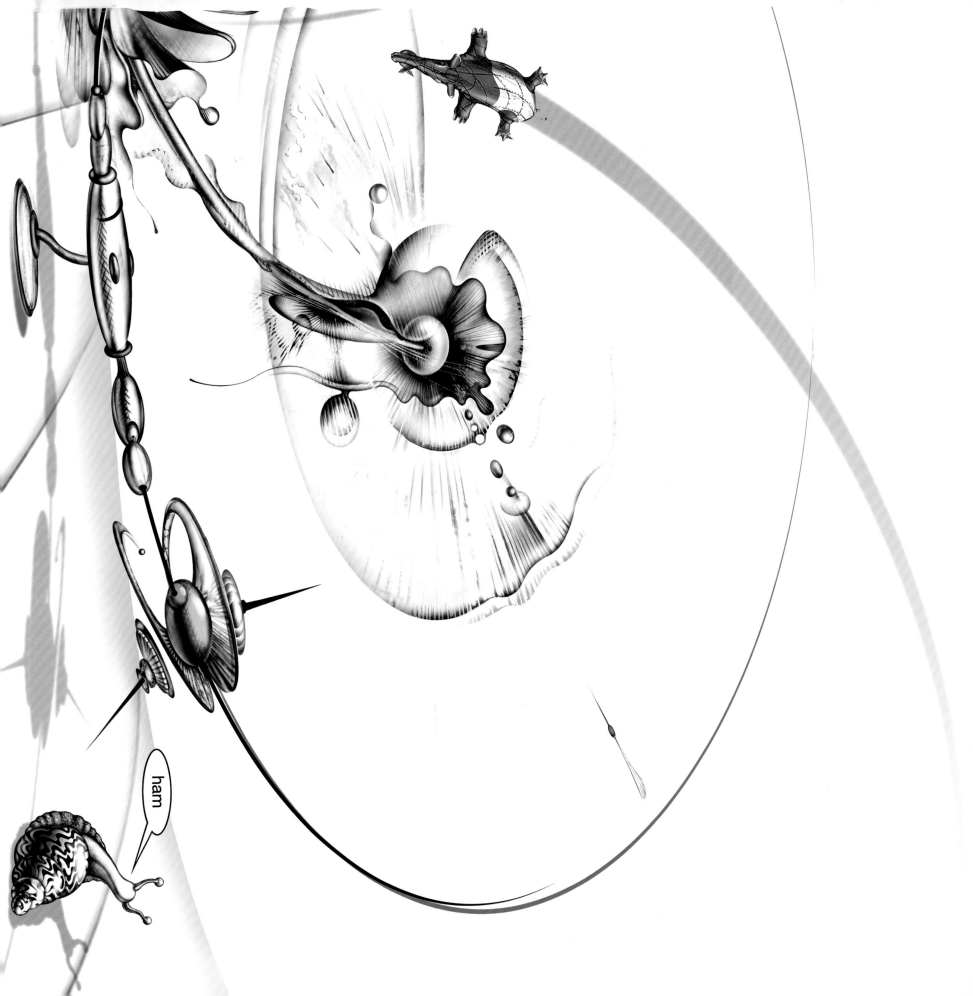